Devils' Pass is published by Stone Arch Books, aCapstone Imprint
1710 Roe Crest Drive
North Mankato, Minnesota 56003
www.mycapstone.com

Library of Congress Cataloging-in-Publication Data is available on the Library of Congress website.

ISBN: 978-1-4965-4989-1 (hardcover)
ISBN: 978-1-4965-4993-8 (ebook pdf)

Summary: Zach Lopez is new to Devils' Pass. He meets the members of the Loyal Order of Helga and soon finds out the town is more than it seems. When a herd of killer unicorns threatens the people of Devils' Pass, Zach and his new friends have to save the town before it's too late.

Editor: Megan Atwood
Designer: Hilary Wacholz

Printed and bound in Canada.
010382F17

DEVILS' PASS

ZACH LOPEZ
VS.
THE UNICORNS OF DOOM

BY JUSTINA IRELAND
ILLUSTRATED BY TYLER CHAMPION

STONE ARCH BOOKS
a capstone imprint

THE LOYAL ORDER OF HELGA

Long, long ago, in a village called New Svalbard, the people who lived there faced unimaginable dangers. A sinkhole as old as time held a door – a portal – to the Otherside, a dark and dreadful place filled with literal nightmares.

To warn travelers of the danger the village posed, the people renamed it Devils' Pass – a reminder to all who lived there and passed through that a darkness sat in the area. A darkness that often had teeth.

For years the people of Devils' Pass endured the danger. Then Helga, one of the white settlers of the village, fell through the cursed sinkhole to the Otherside, coming face-to-face with the terrifying monsters. Helga spent many years there, fighting all sorts of monstrous creatures, learning about their ways and their weaknesses. Through trials and tribulations, and more than a little cunning, she became a fearsome warrior.

Helga fought her way back to Devils' Pass through the portal, now with an understanding of the deadly secrets of the Otherside. Almost immediately, her skills were put to the test. A fearsome frost giant menaced the village, crawling out of the sinkhole and terrorizing the people. Using only a flaming torch, Helga fought the giant and won. It was an astonishing act of bravery – but soon it was clear that the people of Devils' Pass suffered from something else. The sinkhole made the people of the village forget that monsters lived there.

Through some type of magic, however, not all of them forgot. Those who remembered the perils and nightmares the sinkhole brought forth became the Loyal Order of Helga. Along with Helga, the people who remembered the danger vowed to protect Devils' Pass – and the entire world – from the vicious monsters of the Otherside.

CHAPTER ONE
The New Kid in Town

Zach Lopez watched kids walk into Devils' Pass Middle School and sighed.

"This is going to be the worst year of my life," he said, slouching in his seat.

"It won't be that bad," his mother said, putting the car in park and smiling.

Zach gaped at her. Was she serious? "Mom, we just moved to the middle of nowhere, Minnesota, from Los Angeles, I'm starting a brand new school, and, oh, by the way, my mom is the principal." Zach crossed his arms. "This is the worst."

Ms. Lopez laughed and ruffled Zach's hair. He hated when she did that. He smoothed his dark hair back into place and glared at her. She didn't notice. "Well, look on the bright side. I didn't pack your lunch!" she said. Ms. Lopez was terrible at any type of food preparation, something Zach and his younger sister Lisa always joked about. Their family ordered more pizza than anyone else he knew back in L.A. But he wasn't laughing now.

There was nothing funny about starting eighth grade at a new school.

A bell rang, the sound coming from the far-off buildings, and Ms. Lopez startled. "Oh, that's the warning bell. I wanted to be here early, but it looks like that isn't happening. We need to get inside before the final bell. You have your schedule and locker assignment?"

"Yes," Zach said, climbing out of the car and closing the door.

Ms. Lopez got out as well, locking the door and swinging her purse over her shoulder. "Good. You can walk home after school if you don't want to wait for me. Just make sure you don't cut through the park."

Zach frowned. "The park?"

"Yes, one of the teachers warned me that there's a sinkhole in the back of the park. It's fenced off, but she seemed to indicate that there'd been some mischief. Someone was bitten by some kind of animal there last week. It sounds like bad news, so you should probably avoid the park altogether. I don't want you falling in with a bad crowd. Or getting bitten."

Zach rolled his eyes. Ms. Lopez crossed her arms and raised her eyebrows, her Don't Give Me Sass face. Zach raised his hands in surrender. "OK! OK. I'll stay out of the park."

"Good. Now give me a kiss, and get going before you're late for your first day of school."

"Moooooom!"

She tapped her cheek, and Zach sighed. He gave his mom a kiss on the cheek, shrugged on his backpack, and joined the crowd of kids heading into Devils' Pass Middle School.

CHAPTER TWO
Something's Fishy

Devils' Pass Middle School was like Zach's last school. Except the buildings were made of brick instead of stucco, the gym smelled like tater tots because it was connected to the cafeteria by a hallway, and everyone was white with blond hair.

Well, not everyone. But it did seem like a lot of the people had blond hair, and no one was brown like Zach. He wouldn't have noticed it at all, but Brian, a guy in his homeroom, pointed it out. "Is it weird being the only Mexican kid in the school?" he asked.

"I'm not Mexican, I'm Puerto Rican," Zach said, but Brian had already gone back to playing on his phone. It should've been nothing, but for the rest of homeroom, Zach couldn't help but notice that everyone else had pale skin. He felt like even more of an outsider.

Later, as he walked to lunch, Zach's mind began to race, tripping over thoughts of what he would be doing right now if he were still at home, back in L.A.

It was two hours earlier there, so he'd probably be in second period. Last year, his second period class had been math, and he and his friend Seth had spent the year drawing a comic, passing a notebook back and forth and drawing a panel at a time. By the end of the year, they'd had a finished book: *The Adventures of Math Boy*, featuring a superhero with the power of math. It had been such a dork thing to do, but it made the class go by quickly.

He wished he were back in L.A.

He wished his mom hadn't gotten such a great job in the middle of nowhere.

But most of all, he wished his friends were here, so they could draw comics and talk about video games and do everything that wasn't Zach standing alone and awkward in a cafeteria full of people he didn't know.

He got his tray, filled with tacos that looked nothing like L.A. tacos, and sat down at a table at the back of the cafeteria. No one sat with him, and he ate his lunch alone, doodling in his notebook. Zach liked to draw, even though he wasn't very good. To distract himself, he drew pictures of palm trees and a beach with a mermaid sunning herself on a rock.

"Mermaids don't look like that. They have more teeth."

Zach startled as a tall black girl sat on the bench across from him. She set down two trays, one in front of herself and one next to Zach.

"What?" Zach asked as the girl picked up a taco and bit it in half.

"Your mermaid," she said around a mouthful of food, gesturing in the direction of Zach's notebook.

"Needs more teeth."

Zach looked down at his mermaid, who was smiling and wearing a seashell bra, and then back at the girl. She wore a T-shirt that said "I Believe" and her hair was pulled back into an Afro puff. Zach definitely thought she was pretty, but mostly he was relieved to see he wasn't the only brown kid in the entire school.

"They also have claws," a pale blond boy with metal crutches said. He slid in next to Zach, in front of the other tray the girl had carried, before peering over Zach's shoulder at the picture. "Nice palm trees, though."

Zach closed his notebook and stared at the boy and girl. "Who are you?"

"I'm Tiffany," said the girl, "and you're sitting at our table, so don't go getting snippy." She'd already finished her tacos and was noisily drinking her chocolate milk.

"I'm Jeff," the boy said, balancing his crutches against the end of the table. They were different from the ones Zach's friend Domingo got when he broke his leg. These crutches fit around the boy's forearm, and had handles halfway down for the boy's hands. Zach figured that was probably because the boy, Jeff, had to use them all the time. Jeff only had one full leg, the left one shorter and covered by the end of his rolled-up pant leg.

Zach had seen people missing legs before — his Uncle Echo had lost one of his legs while he was fighting the war in Iraq — but Jeff was just a kid. Zach couldn't help but wonder what had happened to his leg.

"And I'm Jeff's sister, Evie," said a girl who sat down next to Tiffany. She was pale, with short, brown hair and freckles. She looked a lot like Jeff, but much younger. Zach wondered if she just looked young for their grade. She asked, "What were we talking about?"

"Mermaids," Tiffany said.

"Oh, ick," Evie said, stabbing at the pile of green beans on her tray and taking a bite. She chewed and swallowed. "All those teeth and claws. Not to mention the slime. Mermaids are so gross."

"The grossest," Tiffany agreed, crushing her milk carton and burping. "So, what's your name, new kid?"

"Zach." He stared, still a little dazed from the conversation's sudden turn. One minute he'd been sitting alone, doodling and feeling sorry for himself, and now he was surrounded by people talking about mermaids as though they were real. "Wait, what makes you think you know exactly what mermaids look like?"

Jeff exchanged a meaningful look with Tiffany and Evie, and all three of them burst into giggles. "Uh, because we've seen one," Jeff said.

"Like, twenty, actually," Tiffany said, stealing a green bean from Evie's plate.

Zach blinked. "What?"

Evie took a bite of a green bean and said, "Yeah, last year the park flooded. The sinkhole overflowed and they were all over the place. Ended up in Mrs. Holtzman's pond, eating her cats. We finally managed to trap them with some macaroni and cheese —"

"Mermaids cannot resist cheese," said Jeff.

" — and left them out in the sun to shrivel up into frogs. It was a rough week," Evie said.

Zach blinked. "Mermaids turn into . . . frogs?"

Tiffany nodded. "If they stay out of the water too long, they shrivel up in the sun. Once they turn into frogs, they're pretty harmless. And they can't change back to mermaids, no matter how wet they get, so we put them back into Mrs. Holtzman's pond."

"I didn't want them to die!" Evie muttered. "And the sinkhole isn't safe."

"Now Mrs. Holtzman has a ton of frogs," Jeff said.

"And no cats," said Evie.

Zach sat in silence for a moment, processing what he'd heard. "Are you guys messing with me?"

Evie shook her head, her eyes wide with surprise. "No, why would we do that?"

"Because I'm the new kid," Zach said. At his last school, they'd often teased the new kids, like the time they'd told a kid from New York that it was against the law to walk on the grass in California. Zach and his friends had laughed as the kid tried to walk from one class to the next, avoiding the grass. He'd thought it was funny back then.

Now, though, he wasn't laughing.

"Maybe he doesn't know that Devils' Pass is where monsters come from," Tiffany said. "Are you going to eat the rest of that?" she asked Jeff. He pushed his tray across the table, and she began eating the remnants of Jeff's tacos.

Zach looked from Tiffany to Evie and finally to Jeff. "Right . . . monsters."

"Yeah, there's a doorway here to another dimension that lets all kinds of weird stuff into town. Immigrants who settled here back in the olden days thought it led to H-E-double hockey sticks, so they called it Devils' Pass," Evie said.

"It's like that old TV show with the vampire slayer chick, but way different," said Tiffany around a mouthful of taco.

Zach didn't know what to say. And he had no idea what show she was talking about. These kids were obviously a few sandwiches short of a picnic. That, or they were jerks. "Look, I don't think it's funny that you're messing with me. And lying about all this stuff. If you didn't want me to sit at your table, all you had to do was say so. I can take a hint."

Tiffany snorted. "Where else were you going to sit, new kid? I don't see anyone else excited to hang out with you."

"Tiff, that's mean," Evie said.

"I don't like being called a liar," Tiffany said, throwing a pointed look at Zach.

Evie put down her fork and frowned at Zach. "You mean you really don't know about the history of Devils' Pass? Didn't you do any research before you came here?"

Zach looked at everyone. They weren't smiling or nudging each other. They didn't look like they were joking at all.

A heavy feeling settled in Zach's stomach, and not from the terrible tacos he'd just eaten.

"Maybe you should tell me about Devils' Pass," Zach said, and waited for what was sure to be an incredible story about his new hometown.

The bell rang, and Jeff nodded. "I'll tell you on the way to class."

CHAPTER THREE
The Otherside of the Story

Everyone grabbed their trays, Evie taking Jeff's as well, and moved to the drop-off window. After they returned their trays, they walked to the hallway. Zach and Evie walked behind Tiffany and Jeff. The hallway was already filling up, so it was easier to maneuver through the crowd that way. Jeff cleared his throat and turned his head so he was speaking to Zach over his shoulder. "OK, so Devils' Pass has always been a really, really strange place."

"Hardly anyone actually knows that for sure, though, because they always forget monster attacks right after they happen," said Evie. "If you'd done research before coming here, you would have found some websites dedicated to talking about the weird things that happen in Devils' Pass. But no one takes the sites seriously." As they walked down the hallway, Zach noticed how everyone waved to Tiffany or Jeff or Evie. So, they couldn't be totally loony; not if most of the school seemed to like them. They waved back, but were way more focused on the story.

Tiffany nodded, turning around and walking backwards. "It's somehow tied to the sinkhole. We call it 'goldfish memory.'"

Jeff continued, "The weirdness goes back to the 1800s, back before settlers decided to build a town here. Back then, the land belonged to the Ojibwe, a Native American tribe. In the early 1830s, the Indian Removal Act was passed. The government came in with guns, and rounded all of the indigenous tribes in Minnesota into reservations to make space for white settlers."

"We still don't have any Ojibwe families in Devils' Pass, but that's just because they're too smart to live in such a weird place. Unlike the rest of us," Tiffany said. Zach was getting the feeling she wasn't any happier about being stuck in the place than he was.

Tiffany stopped walking and grinned at Zach. "Fast forward to 1876, when a group of Scandinavian immigrants come here looking for land. At that time, most of the original settlers, whose ancestors had come from places like England, hated the immigrants because they were different and didn't know English."

"Where I lived in California, a lot of people felt the same way about the Mexican immigrants," Zach said, and Tiffany nodded.

"People are jerks all over," she said, turning around and walking over to her locker. Everyone else paused as well, and Jeff resumed the story while Tiffany got her books for her next class.

"Anyway," Jeff said, "the settlers picked this area, and the town was named New Svalbard, and everyone was happy because they were in their new land.

Everyone except one of the settlers, a woman named Helga."

"Helga is my favorite part," Evie said, leaning in.

Jeff opened his mouth to continue, but Evie started talking instead. "Helga was a big, strapping woman. Town history says she could chop down a tree in less than five minutes. Anyway, Helga's house was near the sinkhole, which at the time everyone thought was a regular pond. For a year, she complained about strange noises and creatures around her pond, but everyone thought it was because she was nervous living by herself. Then one day, she disappeared."

The bell rang, causing Zach to jump. The halls began to empty as everyone hurried to their classes. "So, what happened to Helga?" Zach asked.

"She went to the Otherside," Tiffany said. She said "otherside" like it was a place, like New York or Chicago.

"How do you know that?" Zach asked, his skepticism returning.

"Easy," Jeff said, carefully balancing on his crutches. "Because just when everyone thought she'd died, she came back."

CHAPTER FOUR
Stay Away from Aardvarks

No one wanted to be late to class, so Jeff put the story on pause. "I'll tell you the rest after school," he said, heading down the hallway. Zach had no choice but to go to his next class. He could barely stop fidgeting the rest of the day. He was that excited to find out what would happen next. Zach still didn't quite believe the group of strange kids. Who would? But they were definitely entertaining.

And they were the only kids who had been friendly to him.

After the final bell rang, Zach gathered up all his books and hurried to find Jeff, Tiffany, and Evie to start the trek to the park. The park with the sinkhole. The park his mother had told him to stay out of.

If he got caught, he was going to be in so much trouble. But he HAD to hear the rest of the story. Even though they had World Geography together right after lunch, Tiffany had refused to tell him what happened next. She had been adamant.

"It's Jeff's story," she'd said. "He needs to tell you."

Zach had gotten the feeling that it was less because the story was Jeff's, and more because Tiffany didn't want to tell him.

Zach found the weirdo kids in front of the school near the flagpole. They were huddled in a circle talking, and when he walked up, Tiffany smiled.

"Surprised you showed," she said.

"Why wouldn't I show?" Zach demanded.

"Figured you were chicken," she said, crossing her arms. "Jeff said he told you that the last new kid who came here got eaten by ghost aardvarks. Didn't think you'd stick around."

Zach blinked. "I thought he was joking."

"I wasn't. I was serious," Jeff said, balancing on his crutches as he took off his glasses and wiped them on his shirt. "The things were in the trees, and on moonless nights, they'd drop from the branches and possess people. It was an awful summer."

"Poor Petey," Evie whispered, her eyes swimming with tears. "He was such a nice guy until the aardvarks turned his brain to mush."

Tiffany jerked her head toward the sidewalk. "If we're going, let's get moving. Some of us have extra credit to do."

"It's the first day of school," Zach said.

"So? I take my education seriously," Tiffany responded.

They walked together to the park, keeping a pace Jeff could stick with easily. As they walked, Jeff told the rest of the story.

"After Helga fell into the sinkhole, she was gone for two weeks, but for her, it was years. She came back, talking about a land full of giants and creatures of myth. Everyone thought she was telling stories.

"So there Helga was, dressed in furs that no one had ever seen, with a sword made of a giant tooth strapped to her side, telling a story that no one wanted to believe, when the frost giant came out of the hole right behind Helga and started eating townspeople.

The creature was huge, and people were scared. Helga got a branch, wrapped a kerosene-soaked rag around the end, lit it on fire, and melted the giant. The town was renamed Devils' Pass, as a warning to other folks. There were also rumors that her time on the Otherside changed Helga. Some people even said she was no longer a normal woman, but a Valkyrie," Jeff said.

"And . . . um . . . was she?" Zach asked. He wasn't sure he believed any of this, but he didn't want to make anyone angry. These kids were the only ones who had been even the tiniest bit welcoming. Sure, they'd been a bit annoyed that he'd sat at their table, but overall, they weren't too bad.

Tiffany gave Zach a look he couldn't quite figure out, and shook her head. "Nope, just a regular lady. But after that, she watched over the town, making sure none of the things that came out of the sinkhole hurt anyone. Some other townspeople joined her, and when she died, they named themselves the Loyal Order of Helga, or LOH for short. Helga was Jeff and Evie's great-great-grandma, by the way, and all of us are members of LOH. It's one of the reasons they know so much about the sinkhole and the Otherside."

"What about you? How did you get pulled into this?" Zach asked.

"Because why wouldn't you want to investigate a bunch of super weird things going on? It's like living inside a TV show!" she said.

"Did you grow up here?" Zach asked.

"Naw. My grandma moved us here after my mom died. That's the reason I'm here." Tiffany's tone was sharp, and Zach knew he'd done something to upset her once more.

"So, what brings you to Devils' Pass, Zach?" Evie asked, voice overly bright.

Now it was Zach's turn to frown. "My parents got divorced last year and my mom thought it was a time for a change of scenery for me and my sister."

"Oh, sorry," Evie said. After that, they walked the rest of the way to the park in awkward silence.

The park came into view, and Zach felt certain once again that the weird kids, or the Loyal Order of Helga as they called themselves, were messing with him. The park looked completely normal: playground, green grass, trees. A few people walked their dogs or jogged on the path. If people looked especially nervous — their eyes shifting from side to side — that was just his imagination, wasn't it?

Jeff sat on a park bench with a sigh. "Go ahead and show him. I'm too tired to go all the way to the water," he said, laying his crutches against the bench. Zach couldn't help but stare at the place where Jeff's left leg would be if he had one. His pant leg was rolled up and it was barely noticeable, but Zach found his gaze drawn to the spot. Evie poked him lightly, and when he met her eyes, she shook her head. Zach realized he'd been staring, and looked down at the ground.

"Are you sure?" Evie asked her brother, as though nothing was out of the ordinary.

Jeff nodded. "The sinkhole kind of freaks me out anyway. I'm happy to wait here."

While Jeff waited on the bench, Evie, Tiffany, and Zach walked to the back part of the park.

Everything looked normal, but Zach could swear it got darker as they walked.

CHAPTER FIVE

Still Waters Run Creepy

Finally, they stood in front of a chain-link fence marked with a rusted "No Trespassing" sign. The fence was bent and misshapen at the top, like someone had climbed it and pushed down the mesh. There were holes near the bottom where the fence had been patched, the newer weave shiny against the older, rusty metal. Beyond the fence were grass and then the blackest water Zach had ever seen.

"That's it?" Zach asked. It mostly looked like a normal pond ringed by a busted-down fence.

Tiffany shrugged. "I know it doesn't look like much, but trust us. This place causes a lot of trouble."

Zach stared at the water. Maybe they had been pulling his leg all this time. No way this was a portal to another world or dimension or whatever.

"Watch," Evie said, bending down to pick up a pebble. She threw it over the fence and into the sinkhole, where it landed with a loud plop.

Zach frowned. "It's just a normal pond."

"No, really watch," Tiffany said, picking up another rock and throwing it into the pond. Zach heard the plop, watched the rock sink below the water, and saw the surface of the pond reflect the clouds in the sky above like a mirror.

He blinked. "Where are the ripples?"

Tiffany grinned at him. "Exactly. It isn't a normal pond," she said, throwing another rock. The pond swallowed it with a wet sound, but the surface of the water remained undisturbed.

"That is so weird," Zach said.

"Devils' Pass specializes in weird," Evie said, tossing another rock into the pond.

"Has anyone ever gone in there? Besides Helga, that is?" Zach asked. He wondered what it would be like to climb the fence and dive into the water, to see a whole new world. It was a scary thought, but also kind of exciting.

"Oh, yeah, lots of folks. Only a few go in there willingly, though. The rest have been dragged into the hole by monsters or lured there. Most don't come back," Evie said.

"Recently, only Mr. Hofstrom has come back. He's the town librarian. He fell in there, like, in the 1980s and came back about ten years ago," Tiffany said. "He's also our resident monster expert, and he helps us solve monster problems all of the time. Talk to him and you'll understand why no one is in a hurry to jump into that water."

Zach began to walk, following the jagged line of the chain-link fence. The fence sat a couple of feet from the edge of the pond, and the water was black as ink.

As he stepped over a rock, he saw a flash of pink and blue out of the corner of his eye. He turned toward a nearby stand of trees, but there was nothing there.

"Hey, did you see that?" he called back to the girls.

They looked past him, and Evie shook her head. "I didn't see anything. Let's go back," she called. "Jeff is right, the sinkhole is super creepy." She headed back up the hill to the bench where her brother sat.

Tiffany waited until Zach was next to her to start walking. She said in a low voice, "Hey, try not to stare at Jeff's leg, OK?"

Zach flushed. "I'm sorry. I've never met a kid who was missing a leg before. I was just wondering how he lost it. I mean, was it something from the sinkhole?"

Tiffany shook her head. "No, he was really sick last year. Cancer. They had to do a surgery called a rotationplasty over the summer, so that his foot is where his knee is."

Zach nodded. He had never heard of a rotationplasty, but he had the Internet. He made a note to look it up when he got home. He wanted to learn more about it.

"It's so he can wear a prosthetic leg more easily, but he can't yet because his leg is still healing. If you want to know about Jeff's leg, just ask. He's happy to talk about it," Tiffany said.

Zach swallowed. "Oh. OK. Thanks."

Tiffany looked at him, her gaze direct. "Jeff and Evie are really nice people, and they're my friends." Tiffany's warning was clear: don't hurt them, or else.

Zach swallowed and nodded again, but by then they'd caught up to where Evie was helping Jeff with his crutches. Zach didn't say anything, but stared off toward the sinkhole for a long time. It was just long enough for his embarrassment over staring at Jeff's leg to fade away. The park looked completely normal.

A flash of bright blue and pink caught the corner of his eye again. But one moment it was there, the next it was gone.

Had it really been there at all?

"Hey, Zach, do you want to go with us to get ice cream?" Evie asked.

Zach shrugged. "Sure, if that's OK."

"Of course it's OK." Evie laughed.

Zach looked at Tiffany. She didn't smile, but she wasn't looking at him like he was a bug anymore, either. Maybe that was a good sign?

Suddenly, he felt really tired. But not a bad tired. Because even though he seemed to make Tiffany mad, and quite possibly lived near a portal of doom, he'd maybe found some friends. He smiled all the way to the ice cream shop.

CHAPTER SIX
He Manely Imagined It

Zach was so busy with school that he barely thought about the stuff he'd been told about Devils' Pass. He also wasn't sure he believed that people and cats got eaten all the time by random monsters. If that were true, why hadn't everyone moved away? Even if they did have "goldfish memory," they knew people got hurt, right? None of it made any sense, and by the end of his first week at school, Zach was convinced the weirdo kids just had a strange sense of humor. They were weirdos, after all. Though . . . weirdos he'd had fun getting ice cream with.

Eighth grade was hard, and it seemed like nothing he'd done last year had prepared him. Now, sitting in World Geography, Zach tried to stay awake. It was his least favorite class, especially because he had it with Tiffany, and she knew the answers to almost every question. The class was right after lunch, and the teacher, Mr. Gustaf, had a voice that was exactly the right pitch to make everyone in the room drowsy. The whole class period felt like naptime.

The teacher was discussing capital cities of Scandinavian countries when Zach startled awake. He had fallen asleep, after all — he sat up straight and wiped his mouth. The tiny bit of drool on his hand was proof that he'd made it to dreamland.

He stretched and looked outside the window. Even though it was only the second week of school, already the weather was getting cooler, and the sky was a blue so bright it hurt his eyes.

He wondered what his friends back in L.A. were doing right now. It was probably still super hot there, and that meant everyone would be hanging out at the pool in Zach's best friend Domingo's apartment complex after school. The girls would be wearing their bathing suits and complaining about their new teachers and all the guys would be showing off —

What in the world was that?

Zach blinked. Outside the window was a white horse with a bright pink and green mane. It galloped across the school front lawn and then . . . disappeared.

Zach turned to Tiffany. "Hey, did you see that?" he whispered.

Tiffany looked up from taking notes in her notebook. She looked where Zach pointed out the big windows and straightened, suddenly alert. "Tell me what you saw."

"Mr. Lopez, Miss Donovan. Is there something you'd like to share with the rest of the class?" Mr. Gustaf asked.

Zach felt his face grow hot as everyone in the room turned to look at them. A few kids grinned at the distraction.

Tiffany smiled wide. "No, Mr. Gustaf. Zach was just explaining to me that everyone thinks L.A. or San Francisco is the capital of California, but that Sacramento is really the capital. And I pointed out that's the case with lots of states, such as Pennsylvania, where Pittsburgh and Philadelphia have much larger metropolitan areas and yet Harrisburg is the capital."

Mr. Gustaf adjusted his glasses. "Yes, Miss Donovan, that is true. Great point of discussion."

The teacher went back to the lecture, and Zach mouthed the words "Thank you" to Tiffany. She rolled her eyes and went back to her notes.

Zach was still thinking about the weird horse he'd seen outside the window. He doodled in his notebook, trying to draw the horse exactly as he'd seen it. White body, pink and green mane, golden horn. Not a horse . . . a unicorn? That couldn't be. He thought about the flash of color he'd seen at the sinkhole. Were they related? Was it possible something had come through the portal while they were standing there?

But that would mean that Zach believed that there

really was a hole to another dimension in Devils' Pass. And while Tiffany, Evie, and Jeff seemed on the up and up, Zach still wasn't convinced that they were telling the truth about that. Maybe he'd just seen someone's horse or something. There were farms on the outskirts of town. And he had been dozing off a few minutes before. More than likely he'd dreamed the horse. His eight-year-old sister, Lisa, spent hours watching those magical horse cartoons. His tired brain had probably just imagined a pretty horse outside the window.

That was probably what it was.

Zach was still thinking about the horse (it couldn't have been a unicorn — that was ridiculous) he'd seen, or rather, imagined, when the bell rang. He gathered up his books and filed out of the room with everyone else. In the hallway, Tiffany stopped him.

"Hey, what did you see? Outside the window during class?" she asked.

Zach shook his head. "Nothing. I must've been dozing. Gustaf is so boring."

Tiffany stared at him, her arms full of books. She shifted their weight, and frowned. "Are you sure? This is Devils' Pass, after all. Nothing can turn into something real fast."

"It was nothing," Zach said, his voice a little sharper than he'd intended. "I think I was dreaming or something."

Tiffany widened her eyes and shrugged. "Okaaaaaay. Well, let me know if you want to borrow my notes. My older sister had him last year. She told me his tests count for most of your grade."

"OK," Zach said as Tiffany walked off down the hallway. He turned to head toward his locker and stopped dead when he looked down at the floor.

Right there, in the middle of the floor, was a single, perfect, muddy hoof print.

CHAPTER SEVEN
Tuning In

The next day at lunch, Zach was still thinking about the horse he'd seen, or more likely imagined, during World Geography. He wanted to say something to his friends, to ask if they'd ever seen anything so . . . odd. After all, as Tiffany said, "Devils' Pass specializes in weird." Was this the kind of weird they were talking about?

At the same time, he felt really, really silly even considering it. It was a horse with pink and green hair.

How many horses had pink and green hair? None. Zach had gone home and looked it up on the Internet to be sure. All he found were pictures of people who had dyed their horses' manes and tails. None of them had a golden horn, of course — it must've been someone's runaway horse.

Because otherwise it had to be a unicorn, and that was just . . . crazy.

Zach tried to stop thinking about it. Of course, the more he tried to forget, the more he couldn't. By the time Tiffany and Jeff sat down, Zach was happy for the distraction.

"Anything new?" he asked, taking a big bite of his ham and cheese sandwich. Halfway through the first week of school, Zach decided that cafeteria food wasn't for him, so he'd taken to packing his lunch. He'd brought a PB and J. But it turned out to be a problem because Tiffany was allergic to peanut butter. The day Zach brought the PB and J, she sat at the other end of the table and gave him angry looks. Then in World Geography, she'd told him, "If you want to sit with us, new kid, make sure you don't bring any more murder sandwiches."

Zach took the not-so-subtle hint and asked his mom to buy ham and cheese for his second favorite sandwich. It wasn't as good as peanut butter, but he knew how serious a peanut allergy was. His mom had lectured him about peanut allergies after he'd asked for the ham and cheese. After the talk, Zach felt relieved that nothing had happened to Tiffany because of him. Since then, if it was even possible, Tiffany seemed to trust him less.

Tiffany eyed Zach's sandwich suspiciously as she sat down and said, "So, what's up? You've been looking stressed out all day. Did you see something else weird outside of the window today?"

"Today? Wait, did you see something yesterday?" Jeff asked.

"Zach thought he saw something yesterday during World Geography, but then got freaked out and changed his mind," Tiffany said with a knowing grin.

"No, no, it's nothing. Nothing at all. I didn't see anything." Zach considered telling Tiffany the truth, but what was he supposed to say? "Hey, did you see a magical horse yesterday while Mr. Gustaf was going over Scandinavian capitals?"

"Are you sure?" Jeff asked.

Zach nodded. "Yeah, yeah, I'm sure."

"We're asking because Mason Briggs has gone missing," Tiffany said, serious once more. "He's the third person this week to disappear. His mom went to get him up for school and all she found was a bed full of glitter and his footprint outside in the front yard."

Jeff said, his voice solemn, "When people start disappearing, it's usually a good sign that some monster is hanging out in town."

Zach's heart began to pound and his palms got super sweaty. He didn't like lying, but he also couldn't believe that there were monster unicorns kidnapping kids. None of this made any kind of sense.

"Where's Evie?" Zach asked, after a long,

uncomfortable silence. A change of subject was definitely in order.

"Evie is in the library, freaking out," Jeff said, moving around a pile of what looked like tuna noodle casserole on his tray. "She doesn't think she belongs here, and she keeps saying that coming here was a big mistake."

"What does that mean?" Zach asked. "A mistake to go to school?"

"Evie is almost two years younger than us. She skipped a grade. She's super smart," Tiffany said, eating the rest of the food on her tray. She looked at Jeff's tray and smiled as he slid it over to her without a word.

"She's been super stressed. Last year she was in fifth grade and now she's in seventh. She doesn't want to let everyone down," Jeff said. "So, she's going to start studying through lunch."

"I told her it's totally not necessary. She's psyching herself out," Tiffany said. "But she is really nervous about a test tomorrow. She needs to eat, though."

"Could you take her lunch?" Jeff asked Tiffany. "I have to go to the counselor's office to talk over some things." He made a face.

Tiffany shook her head, and scraped the last of the casserole from Jeff's tray into her mouth. "Can't. I have student council."

"Student council?" Zach asked.

"Yeah, I'm the student council president." Tiffany grinned. She stacked Jeff's tray on top of her own. "

Zach cleared his throat. "If you guys don't mind, I can take Evie her lunch." It was a perfect distraction. Not to mention, he could do something nice for people who were starting to become his friends.

Jeff and Tiffany looked at each other, seemingly impressed. Jeff nodded. "That would be awesome. Gladys, the lunch lady, usually makes one vegetarian sandwich a day just for Evie."

Tiffany grinned. "That's a great idea. Plus, you could help Evie study. She won't feel as embarrassed around you, since you're new."

Zach blushed. It felt nice to know that Tiffany approved of his idea.

She waved and left, and Jeff climbed to his feet, balancing on his crutches. "Tiff's right. And Evie is probably starving. She usually brings a snack to school, but she never misses lunch. If you want, I'll go with you and put in Evie's lunch number before I go to the counselor's."

"No, it's cool. I can get it." Zach said. He could handle this. This was a normal thing to think about.

As he walked to the lunch line, a kid passed by him in a daze and got into line in front of him. There was glitter all over his hair and backpack. It seemed weird to see someone with so much glitter on them. There were no parties in September, as far as he knew. Maybe it was the kid's birthday.

"Hey, happy birthday," Zach said.

The kid turned around, his expression spacey. "It's not my birthday." He looked past Zach as if he was watching a movie right behind him.

"Oh, sorry, I saw the glitter and thought it was your birthday," Zach said.

"What glitter?" the kid asked. He turned back around and started humming a creepy tune: DEE da DEE, DEE da DEEEEE. It was like Zach wasn't there anymore.

He thought about telling the kid that he was covered in rainbow glitter, but decided against it. He didn't know him. Maybe he was being sarcastic.

There was a single vegetarian sandwich in the lunch line (made with hummus instead of turkey), and Zach paid for it and a soy milk before heading to the library. There, he found Evie sitting at a table in the study area, head bent over an English book, reading a story and scowling.

"Hey," Zach said softly. "I brought you lunch." He didn't see the librarian anywhere, but there was no use in risking a scolding.

Evie looked up and smiled. "Hey, Zach. Thanks. I am starving!"

Zach sat down across from Evie and watched as she opened up the wrapper and scarfed down the sandwich. There were dark circles under her eyes, and her hair was pulled back into a messy ponytail. As Tiffany had said, she looked stressed.

"Are you OK? Do you want to talk about it?" Zach asked. He wasn't a genius, but he knew what it felt like to struggle in school.

Evie sighed and shrugged. "I feel like maybe I made a mistake skipping a grade. Everything is a lot harder than I expected. When the teachers told me that my test scores were good enough to skip, I thought it would be cool. But now . . . I'm really worried about this first test." She rested her head in her hands. "What if I'm not smart enough to do this?"

Zach awkwardly patted Evie's shoulder. He said, "My mom has worked for a school for as long as I can remember, and one of the things I know is that they don't let you skip a grade unless you're really, really smart. You've got this, Evie. Don't freak yourself out, you know?"

Evie nodded, head still in her hands. She looked as miserable as she had when Zach walked in.

Zach was getting the feeling that maybe he wasn't so good at pep talks.

Neigh.

Zach turned toward the sound, looking left and then right. Evie hadn't moved. And as loud as the sound was, there was no way she wouldn't have heard it.

Maybe he'd imagined it.

Neigh, SNORT.

The sound came again, and Zach jumped to his feet. Evie sat up and looked at him.

"What's wrong?" she asked.

"Didn't you hear that?" Zach asked.

"Hear what?" Evie furrowed her brows.

"It sounded like a horse," he said, walking toward the tall shelves of books. He ducked down one aisle and then another, but they were all empty. After about five minutes, Zach realized he and Evie were the only people in the library.

But he knew he'd heard a horse. No way he'd just imagined the noise.

Zach came back to where Evie sat. "Why would there be a horse in the library?" she asked, frowning at him. He suddenly realized how silly he must seem, looking for a horse in the school library of all places.

"It's just, I keep thinking I see this horse with rainbow hair, and . . . you know what, never mind. Why don't I help you study?" he said.

Evie laughed, and shook her head. "I'm tired of studying. Why don't we go outside in the sun and eat lunch? It's a really nice day outside. Don't you think?" Then she hummed DEE da DEE, DEE da DEEEEE. She stared off into space.

Zach frowned. There was that creepy tune again. The same one the kid in the cafeteria had hummed. Even weirder, this wasn't like Evie at all. She had just been stressing out so much that she forgot to eat.

"Are you sure?" he asked her. "I thought you were worried about the test."

Evie shrugged. "Eh, I'll either do well on it or I won't. Come on, let's hurry before lunch is over."

"But you were super worried . . ." Zach trailed off. Evie only smiled, and Zach half smiled back, still incredibly confused. But she picked up her empty sandwich wrapper and soy milk carton from the table, so Zach grabbed his backpack. He decided she must really, really need a break.

As he walked behind Evie, he noticed something on her backpack. "Hey, it looks like you have glitter all over your back," he said.

"Really? That's weird. Someone must've gotten it on the chair," she said, shrugging. She walked ahead of Zach, humming the strange tune and skipping along down the hallway.

As he walked out of the library, Zach looked over his shoulder, expecting to see another quick flash of rainbow-colored hair.

But it was still empty, and Zach wondered just exactly what was going on.

CHAPTER 8

Staying in the Road Is Dangerous

On his way home from school, Zach couldn't stop thinking about the glitter. First the kid in the cafeteria, and then Evie. It was almost like the glitter meant something important. He stopped walking when he heard something familiar.

"DEE da DEE, DEE da DEEEEE."

Zach looked out in the road, where a girl he didn't recognize stood right in the middle. She had blond hair and her white sweatshirt was covered in glitter. She was humming — and it was that same creepy song again.

"Hey, are you OK?" Zach called. It seemed strange for someone to walk down the middle of Main Street.

The street was the busiest road in all of Devils' Pass, and the way she walked made Zach think maybe she wasn't feeling OK.

"DEE da DEE, DEE da DEEEEE," the girl hummed, as though she hadn't heard Zach.

"You should probably get out of the street," Zach said. The girl kept walking.

Zach hesitated. He considered getting the girl out of the road. But she looked older than him, and it seemed like she knew what she was doing. Maybe she had a reason.

He shrugged and started walking home again. He'd only gone a little way when he heard the squeal of brakes and a horn honking for a very long time before a woman screamed.

Zach spun around. An older lady climbed out of a car that had stopped in the middle of Main Street. She turned to Zach.

"Call 911," she said. "I think I hit her!"

Zach fumbled into his pocket and pulled out the

cell phone that his mom had given him. She'd told him that it was only for emergencies. This was definitely an emergency.

People from up and down Main Street ran out of their shops. Zach tried texting his mom, but she didn't answer. He didn't know what else to do, so he watched helplessly as people stood near the girl, yelling directions. After what seemed like years, an ambulance finally arrived and the paramedics gathered up the girl on a stretcher. They'd put a huge brace around her neck, but Zach couldn't see much else. The old lady could not be consoled and Zach heard a shop owner say, "Who knows why she was in the middle of the street? It wasn't your fault."

Zach felt shaky. He really wished his mom would text him back. One of the shop owners on Main Street saw the look on his face and offered to give him a ride home. Zach politely declined. Devils' Pass was a small town, but he still didn't know the man.

When he got home, Zach collapsed on the couch. He tried texting his mom again, but there was still no answer. He turned the TV on to try to forget seeing the girl lying on the ground. But no matter how much he tried to think of something else, his brain kept coming back to the squeal of brakes and the creepy song the girl was humming.

Zach was halfway through the third episode of *Gem War Attack* — the one where the secret identity of the evil queen is revealed — when he heard the front door close. He looked up to see his mom and Lisa walk in, both laughing.

"Hey," Zach said, looking at the clock. It was nearly six-thirty, past dinnertime. "Where have you guys been?" He still felt a little panicky because of the girl in the road, but his worry about her was now replaced by worry for his mom and Lisa.

"Oh," Ms. Lopez said, smiling. "I decided to go for a walk in the park. It was such a beautiful day. Seemed like a waste not to enjoy it."

"I went to the park too," Lisa said. "Do you know the playground has one of those things where you can run in a circle and spin it around?"

"The merry-go-round?" Zach asked.

"Yes!" Lisa said. "Anyway, it's super fun! I played on that for a while and then I played on the swings."

"Those spinny things make you sick," Zach said. "And you hate swings. You always say you're afraid that they might flip over."

Lisa stared at Zach for a minute, and then she shrugged and laughed. "Whatever. It was awesome."

"I texted you," Zach said to his mom. He stared at her pointedly.

She shrugged. "I lost my phone. How silly!" she said with a laugh.

Ms. Lopez and Lisa walked farther into the living room. Zach's eyes widened. There was a long bloody scrape on Lisa's knee, and blood ran down her leg. "Lisa! What happened to your knee?"

She glanced down at it and laughed. "I don't know, I guess I might have tripped."

"It's only a scrape, Zach," said Ms. Lopez. "Don't freak out about it."

Zach frowned at his mom and sister. This was nothing like them. His mom hated being outside because her allergies went haywire from the pollen. And Lisa had been on the Internet every night since they'd gotten to Minnesota, talking to her friends back in L.A. There was no way his mom wouldn't run to get the antibacterial spray at the first sign of a scrape. And she would never say, "Don't freak out about it." That alone made Zach feel freaked out.

Something weird was definitely going on, but Zach decided to change the subject. There were too many things to be worried about at the moment.

"Should I order a pizza or something?" he asked.

Lisa and his mother stood in the entryway, barely moving.

"Actually, I'm not that hungry. I think I'll go sit in the backyard and look at the grass," Ms. Lopez said, walking through the house.

"I'm coming too," Lisa said, following Ms. Lopez into the backyard. Zach watched as his sister and mother walked outside. As they passed by, he heard them humming, "DEE da DEE, DEE da DEEEEE." Through the sliding glass door that led to the back patio he could see them walk to the middle of the lawn. They sat down on the grass, and closed their eyes, serene smiles on their faces, still humming the creepy song.

Something caught Zach's eye. He saw glitter all over his mom and Lisa — just like the spacey kid in the cafeteria. Like Evie in the library.

And now, just like Evie, his mom and sister didn't seem to care about anything but being outside.

Something weird was definitely going on.

CHAPTER 9

There Have Been Better Days

The next morning when Zach went down to breakfast, he was surprised to find his mother sitting in her bathrobe, drinking coffee and humming, "DEE da DEE, DEE da DEEEEE" as she stared out the window.

"Hey, we need to leave soon. It's almost seven o'clock," Zach said, his worry from last night stronger than ever. Usually when he came down to breakfast, his mom was dressed and ready to go, her foot tapping impatiently while she waited for him to grab a cereal bar. But today she was super chill, not at all like herself.

"I think I'm going to take a sick day," she said.

"But you never take a sick day," Zach said. Last year his mom had gotten the flu, and rather than stay home, she'd gone to work, a paper bag tucked into her purse in case she had to throw up while she was stuck in traffic on the freeway.

But here she was today, not a care in the world, and happier than Zach had ever seen her. And she was still covered in glitter. His mom hated glitter because it made a huge mess. Nothing made sense, and it was making Zach's stomach hurt.

His mother continued humming. The song was flat and toneless, less of a song and more of the kind of weird, constant buzz a bug might make. Just listening to it made him want to run in the opposite direction.

He walked across the kitchen and opened the cupboard to get a cereal bar.

Rainbow glitter drifted and swirled across the counter, driven by an unseen breeze. Zach looked around. There was glitter all over the kitchen table, the counter, even the floor. The glitter in his mom's hair sparkled like she'd just gotten back from a party.

"Where'd all this glitter come from?" he asked, his unease growing even more.

Ms. Lopez looked around and frowned. "I don't know. I didn't even know it was here."

Zach carefully grabbed a cereal bar from the cupboard, trying not to touch the glitter. He didn't know how, but it seemed bad. He grabbed his backpack and ran out the front door. He was going to be late. He had to get going.

He slammed the door and locked it, and then turned around fast. Right outside the front door, his sneakers splashed in a puddle, and he realized that it had rained again overnight. But that wasn't the most surprising sight.

There, in the middle of the yard, was a horse with a golden horn.

Not a horse. A unicorn.

It looked like every unicorn on TV and in the movies: a large white horse with a pink and blue striped mane and tail. In the middle of its head, a golden-spiraled horn narrowed to a point. It was absolutely beautiful.

Zach froze. The unicorn hadn't noticed him, and he wasn't quite sure what to do. It tossed its head and a cloud of glitter filled the air, sparkling in the early morning sunshine. The glitter drifted and fell to the ground a few inches away from the toe of Zach's tennis shoes. Where it hit the ground, it sparked, like fireworks. He thought about the glitter in the house.

What would happen if that glitter touched him?

At least now he knew where all the glitter came from. Lisa and his mom must've run into the unicorn at some point, gotten glitter all over themselves, and then spread the glitter all over the house.

Zach shook his head. "Zach, you don't really believe this, do you?" he whispered to himself. Here he was looking at a real-life unicorn, and still he couldn't believe it was real.

But it was real. Too real.

Zach thought of poor Petey, who had been

possessed by the ghost aardvarks and had his brain scrambled and died. Somehow, he didn't think the unicorn wanted to possess him, so then what?

The unicorn shook its mane again, glitter sparkling everywhere. Zach thought of his mom, Evie, and the spacey boy in the cafeteria. Somehow, the glitter made people not care. He was sure of it.

He definitely didn't want the glitter touching him. He jumped back to avoid a few sparkles that drifted too close.

Zach's sudden movement got the unicorn's attention, and it looked up. When it saw him, it snorted, and Zach's earlier unease grew into something much, much bigger.

"Uh, hey, horsey," Zach said. Could unicorns understand English?

The unicorn's ears flattened and the creature snarled at Zach, baring its teeth. Zach took a step back, and another. His heart pounded in his chest and his palms got so sweaty that he dropped his cereal bar.

Instead of regular, flat, horse teeth, the unicorn had super pointy shark teeth.

LOTS and LOTS of super pointy shark teeth. Three rows of teeth, to be exact.

Zach decided now was a good time to freak out.

He turned around to his front door, but the door was locked and he'd already stuck the key in his backpack. Behind him came the sound of hoofbeats as the unicorn charged him.

Zach dove into the evergreen bushes next to his front stoop. The unicorn's horn pierced the front door, lodging deep into the wood. The unicorn whinnied in rage as Zach climbed out of the bushes.

As the unicorn fought to pull its horn out of the front door, Zach turned and ran down the sidewalk and out into the street, glancing over his shoulder to see if the unicorn would follow him. He really hoped it wouldn't.

It did.

Part of his brain refused to acknowledge what

he was seeing. Surely this wasn't really happening. A
unicorn with jagged teeth was not really chasing him,
snorting puffs of steam into the cool morning air,
glitter flying in its wake.

Because unicorns were not real.

The unicorn snarled and lunged for Zach, the
pointy teeth ripping through his backpack. For a
moment, he struggled, the creature's breath hot on the
back of his neck. Zach flailed, his arms coming out of
the shoulder straps of the backpack.

One moment the unicorn was about to take a bite
out of him, the next he was free, sprinting down the
street toward school.

A unicorn had tried to eat him.

This was the worst Tuesday ever.

After a couple of blocks, Zach realized that the
unicorn wasn't following him. He slowed down to a
walk, a side stitch making him grimace. He wondered
if his mom and sister were safe inside the house?
Why had the unicorn tried to attack him, but not them?

He thought about going back to see if they were OK. He also thought about all the homework he'd lost. He couldn't believe the unicorn had his backpack. Did unicorns eat homework, or was that only dogs? None of his teachers were ever going to believe this.

He wasn't even sure he believed it.

CHAPTER TEN
All That Glitters . . . IS BAD

Zach headed straight to Tiffany's locker once he got to school. Thanks to his terrified sprint, he was earlier than usual, and the halls were mostly empty. Tiffany's locker was at the opposite end of the hallway from Zach's. He passed a few kids leaning against their lockers, including Brian, the boy from his homeroom. They all stared into space and hummed the same terrible tune that Evie and his mom had been humming. Brian's sweatshirt was covered with glitter, so Zach made a wide circle around him.

The glitter was bad news.

But the glitter was also EVERYWHERE. It was on the lockers, on the floor, sparkling and glinting. Zach hopped from floor tile to floor tile, trying to avoid it. What would happen if it touched his skin?

He didn't want to find out.

Zach jogged down the hall, avoiding the deepest piles of glitter, until he saw Tiffany. She leaned against her locker, reading a book on alien abductions and eating an apple. Zach's stomach growled and he thought longingly of his dropped cereal bar. Tuesday was turning out to really stink.

"Hey, I need to talk to you," Zach said. He glanced up and down the hall, suddenly worried that maybe the unicorn was going to appear and try to eat his face or something.

Tiffany glanced over the top of her book. "What's up? You look stressed."

"A unicorn tried to eat me this morning," Zach said.

Tiffany lowered her book and stood up straight. "Did you just say . . . a unicorn?"

"Yes! Haven't you seen the piles of glitter everywhere?" Zach knew he sounded panicky and out of control, but he couldn't help it. Yesterday he'd seen a girl get hit by a car, and today he'd been attacked by a unicorn with shark teeth. It really was just a good time to panic.

Tiffany shrugged. "I did, but I figured maybe it was someone's birthday or something. Glitter bombs, you know?"

Zach said, "I guess," and then quickly filled Tiffany in on everything that had happened: the flash of rainbow hair near the sinkhole, the weird horse outside during World Geography and in the library, people covered in glitter and humming, the girl in the road getting hit by the car, and finally, that morning's events.

"It ate my backpack. It had shark teeth," Zach whispered, feeling tired now that his fear was starting to fade a little. "You probably don't even believe me." He waited for her to say that he'd imagined it, that there were no such thing as unicorns.

But she didn't.

"Oh, I believe you," Tiffany said. She pointed to Zach's hoodie and he craned his neck to see his back, finally taking the sweatshirt off. What he saw made his stomach sick.

There was a jagged tear in the hood of his sweatshirt. The unicorn had eaten part of his hoodie.

He was also covered in glitter.

"Ahh, get it off, get it off!" Zach said, trying to brush the glitter off his back. As he did, the piles in the hallway drifted and swirled in big lazy circles, coating his pant legs as well.

"Zach, you aren't going to be able to get rid it. Glitter is like the pink eye of crafting supplies," Tiffany said, rolling her eyes.

"What?"

"Once it's on one person, it's on everyone," Tiffany said, looking at Zach like she couldn't believe she'd been stuck with such a moron.

"But isn't it the glitter that's making everyone spacey and weird?" Zach pointed down the hall, where everyone was kind of doing nothing and staring off into space.

A thoughtful expression came over Tiffany's face and she tapped her chin. "It could be that some people have a natural immunity to the glitter. I mean, I'm covered in it as well, and I feel fine."

Zach settled down and leaned against the lockers. "This is so messed up. Unicorns are supposed to grant wishes, not make people mindless," he moaned.

Tiffany shook her head and patted him reassuringly on the arm. "Nothing that comes from the Otherside is good," she said, finishing her apple and tossing the core into a nearby trash can. "Come on, we need to get Evie and Jeff. This is going to get really bad, really fast."

The two of them made their way down the hallway to Jeff's locker. Tiffany frowned. "Like, half the school is missing. Where is everyone?"

"Home? When I left this morning, my mom was acting like it was a weekend or something, just hanging out drinking coffee," Zach said.

Tiffany tapped her chin. "So the glitter makes people spaced out? Just kind of, not stressed and carefree? That's probably why that girl got hit by the car. She wasn't thinking about how dumb it is to stand in the middle of the road."

"Yep," Zach said, pointing to where a girl lay in a patch of sunshine in the hallway, smiling with her eyes closed. "Like I said, spacey. But . . . worse than spacey. My sister and mom weren't even eating yesterday."

Tiffany nodded. "Yeah. And add some chick getting hit by a car . . . this seems a little more dangerous. A lot more dangerous, in fact."

They reached Jeff's locker. Jeff balanced on his crutches while he grabbed books from his locker. A thick layer of glitter surrounded him in a semi-circle.

"Jeff," Tiffany called. "We've got a situation."

He turned around and sighed. "What is up with all the glitter?"

"Evil unicorns from the Otherside are using it to make everyone lazy. Or 'spacey' as Zach calls it,"

Tiffany said. "We think part of the reason we aren't affected is a natural immunity, but we're not sure. So try not to touch it."

"Too late. I stepped in it on my way into the building. My crutches are covered. Maybe it isn't an immunity. It could be the Loyal Order of Helga working its magic." Jeff looked at Tiffany meaningfully.

Zach's eyes widened. "Wait, what do you mean, the Loyal Order's magic? You guys have magic powers?"

Tiffany shook her head. "We don't know how it works. Only that sometimes things don't affect us like they do everyone else. Like how we always remember the monsters that attacked the town when no one else does. It's really wonky."

Zach thought about that for a second. It meant that . . . maybe he was part of the Order now? He shook his head. No time to think about that. But he was surprised at how much he wanted it to be true.

Jeff threw his books back into the locker and slammed it shut. He then used his crutches to swing over the glitter to a cleaner spot on the floor. The ends of his crutches and his feet were a sparkly green, but he seemed fine.

"Well, I guess I don't have to worry about that English quiz today," Jeff said with a small laugh.

Tiffany pointed to the locker next to Jeff's. "Where's Evie?"

"At home. She told my mom that she wanted to stay home and watch butterflies. Mom thought that was a great idea. She even canceled the showings she had scheduled," Jeff said.

"Oh, no!" Tiffany exclaimed. "That means Evie and your mom must be infected. This just keeps getting worse."

"Yeah," Jeff said. "Evie refused to eat her cocoa snaps this morning. I put the cereal in her favorite bowl and everything to try to get her to eat them."

She shook her head. "Not good." To Zach, Tiffany

said, "Jeff and Evie's mom is a real estate agent. She has posters for her agency all over town. She's super busy, and she never cancels a showing. Evie loves cocoa snaps, plus she had her test today. No way she would miss that on her own."

Jeff's eyes widened. "So, they're definitely not immune."

Zach sighed. "Now I see what you mean by the Loyal Order's magic being wonky." He patted Jeff's shoulder. "My mom and sister are infected too." Jeff shot him a sympathetic look.

Tiffany stood up straight and pointed to the doors. "We need to get to the library. This is a problem that is Mr. Hofstrom-level."

"Mr. Hofstrom? You mean the guy who visited the Otherside?" Zach asked.

Jeff nodded and Tiffany led the way out the door. Zach followed, feeling the tiniest bit better. This sounded like a plan.

At least someone would know what to do.

CHAPTER ELEVEN

Old Notebooks Are Rad

The Devils' Pass Public Library was a few blocks from the middle school. As the trio made its way there, they saw a lot more people who'd been affected by the unicorns. They were sitting or lying in their yards looking up at the clouds passing by overhead. Everyone looked happy, and Zach wondered if maybe he'd overreacted. Could something that made everyone so happy really be that bad?

But then Zach thought about the unicorn's teeth, pointed and crooked like a shark's, and decided that anything with teeth like that probably wasn't up to any good. Not to mention the fact that people weren't eating and were getting hit by cars.

As they walked, Zach got nervous again. Glitter was scattered here and there — pretty much everywhere now — rainbow, green, blue, pink, silver.

The library came into view, an old-fashioned building with columns and fancy shrubbery. It looked like a library you'd see in a movie: brick, with DEVILS' PASS PUBLIC LIBRARY carved into the front lintel over the doors. According to the sign posted on the door, the library didn't open for another two hours, but Jeff made his way over to a buzzer next to the book return and pushed it three times, very quickly.

"Mr. Hofstrom lives at the library," Tiffany explained. "We have a secret code for when something like this happens."

"Oh, now I remember that old TV show you were talking about. It is like Buf—" Zach started.

"It isn't," Tiffany said, not bothering to look at him.

Zach thought about all the spacey people and the unicorn's sharp teeth tearing into his backpack. And how dangerous that might be. "How often does something like this happen?"

"A lot," Jeff said.

That did not make Zach feel good.

There was a popping sound as the lock disengaged, and the main door swung open. Jeff led the way, Tiffany and Zach close behind. Zach was relieved to see that there wasn't any glitter inside the foyer of the library. They were safe from the unicorns. For now.

They walked into the main room of the library. There were a few computers, a counter, a set of stairs going down with a velvet rope, and a sign that read EMPLOYEES ONLY. And stacks and stacks of books. But no Mr. Hofstrom.

"What's come from the sinkhole this time?" a voice behind them asked. Zach turned to see a black man walking up the stairs. Zach had been expecting someone old, but Mr. Hofstrom looked younger than

Zach's mom, who had turned thirty-six last year. He was completely bald and wore a sweatshirt with a t-shirt under it, and a pair of sweatpants. He looked like he was about to go running. It was chilly in the library, though, and if he lived in the building it was no wonder he was bundled up.

"Unicorns. With pointy teeth," Zach said, when Jeff and Tiffany looked at him.

"Of course they have pointy teeth! They're unicorns." The man reached into his pocket and pulled out a pair of glasses. After he put them on, he pointed at Zach. "Do I know you?"

"This is Zach Lopez, Mr. H. He just moved to Devils' Pass," Tiffany said.

He looked Zach up and down before turning back to Tiffany and Jeff. "So, the town's got unicorns? Let's fix this."

Mr. Hofstrom led the way to a back room marked EMPLOYEES ONLY and unlocked the door. Inside was a desk with a computer, various cabinets, bookshelves, and a mini-fridge in the corner. Zach's stomach growled loudly, and Mr. Hofstrom looked at him.

"Have you eaten?" he asked Zach.

"No, sir. The unicorn ate my backpack and I dropped my breakfast," Zach said, feeling like he'd done something wrong even though he was pretty sure he hadn't.

"Sir? I'm definitely not a sir. Call me Hoff or Mr. H." Mr. Hofstrom went to a cupboard and pulled down a box of granola bars. He tossed the box to Tiffany and said, "I'm going to get my notebook. Those are peanut-free, Tiff, so have at them. Jeff, awesome sticker on your crutches, man. But what's up with all the glitter?"

"Unicorns," Jeff said.

"Oh, right, right. Just a sec." Mr. Hofstrom walked out of the room and Tiffany grabbed the box, opening it up and tossing a granola bar to Zach. When she offered one to Jeff, he shook his head and she stuck the bar in her back pocket, opening another one and taking a big bite out of it. Zach opened his own bar and ate it too fast. Now that he was no longer in immediate danger, he was really, really hungry.

"That was Mr. Hofstrom?" Zach asked.

Tiffany nodded. "Yup."

"I thought Mr. Hofstrom would be a lot older," Zach said.

Tiffany nodded. "He is. He was a teenager in the 1980s. But the sinkhole is weird, and when he came back ten years ago, he still looked like a teenager."

"He skipped like twenty years of stuff," Jeff said, sinking into a chair next to a filing cabinet.

"He got the librarian job because Mayor French wanted someone who could keep a record of all the things that happen," Tiffany said. "Remember when we told you about goldfish memory?"

Zach nodded. "Because goldfish don't remember things."

"Exactly. We think it might be because of the sinkhole," Jeff said. "Mayor French and Mr. H are the only adult members of the Loyal Order of Helga. Everyone else gets goldfish memory. Mr. H. doesn't leave the library, so he's great at keeping track of everything that happens."

"Why isn't he affected by goldfish memory?" Zach asked, eyeing the box of granola bars and wondering if it would be rude if he ate another one.

"Don't know. The Mayor thinks it's the LOH magic protecting me," Mr. Hofstrom said. "He knows about the Loyal Order of Helga, right?" he asked Tiffany. She nodded through a huge bite of granola bar.

Mr. Hofstrom had walked back into the room carrying a cup of coffee and a dirty notebook. It was like nothing Zach had ever seen. Plastic, with a flap that folded over to keep the notebook closed, it looked like an envelope. There was a picture of a red sports car on the front, and on the spine were the words "Trapper Keeper." Zach wondered if it was some kind of magical book, but before he could ask, Mr. Hofstrom made his way behind the desk and sat down.

"Before we get started, Zach, let me tell you the

awesome story of how I ended up in the other place,"
Mr. Hofstrom said.

Zach took a deep breath and then let it out. They
didn't have time for stories — his mom and sister and
who knew who else could be in danger.

But he had the feeling that he didn't have a choice.

CHAPTER TWELVE
If You've Seen One Unicorn . . .

Tiffany cleared her throat. "Maybe another time, Mr. H? We've got quite the unicorn situation. Both Zach's and Jeff's moms and sisters are probably in danger."

Mr. Hofstrom adjusted his glasses. "Right, right, my bad. Rain check, Zach. You don't want to hear about me, you want to learn how to stop the unicorn herd."

"It's not a herd, just one," Zach said, and Mr. Hofstrom laughed.

"It's more than just one. Unicorns never travel by themselves, they travel in a herd. So even though you only saw one doesn't mean it was the only one in town." Mr. Hofstrom opened his notebook, turning pages until he came to a picture of a unicorn and notes written on notebook paper. "So, here we go. Unicorns usually travel in packs of ten or more. They're invisible to humans and can only be seen in the presence of water or mud."

"Like, standing in the mud?" Tiffany asked.

Mr. Hofstrom shrugged. "Doesn't say."

"My grass was wet this morning when I saw the unicorn, so I'm guessing they have to be standing on it," Zach said.

Mr. Hofstrom pointed at Zach and gave him a wink. "Good to know. Anyhoo, their horns emit a glitter that affects humans' survival instinct." Mr. Hofstrom looked up from the page, his expression serious. "They basically happy folks to death."

"Wait, to death?" Zach thought of his mom, smiling and drinking her coffee. His heart began to pound. He couldn't let her die.

"Don't worry, we're not going to let it get to that point," Mr. Hofstrom said, patting Zach on the arm. "That only happens after prolonged exposure to the glitter. The sparkle ponies wait until their victims have gone into a permanent blissful state before they feed."

Tiffany made a choked noise. "The unicorns are going to . . . eat everyone?"

Mr. Hofstrom nodded. "Why do you think they have such pointy teeth?"

"But one chased me this morning," Zach said. "They weren't waiting for me to be happy."

Mr. Hofstrom nodded again. "Probably because they could see that the glitter didn't work on you. Some people are immune. Unicorns use the horn on those people."

Tiffany frowned. "So, it isn't Loyal Order of Helga magic protecting us?"

Mr. Hofstrom shrugged. "Could be. Or you could have a natural immunity. That's the thing about magic, it isn't science. Either way, it's a good thing, right?"

Zach couldn't help but feel a little disappointed about that. Maybe he wasn't a part of the group after all . . .

"Wait, you said sometimes unicorns use their horns. What's the horn do?" Zach asked.

"It's pointy, right?" Mr. Hofstrom shot him a knowing look.

Zach's eyes widened and he remembered how the unicorn had driven its horn into the front door. "Oh, man," he whispered.

"So, how do we stop them?" Jeff asked. His face was flushed with worry, and Zach wondered if he was thinking of his mom and Evie. Just like Zach was thinking of his own mom and sister. They had to stop the unicorns and save the town. There was no other option.

Mr. Hofstrom flipped a few pages, reading quietly. Zach shifted from foot to foot nervously, and Tiffany chewed on her thumbnail. What if there was no way to stop the unicorns?

Mr. Hofstrom tapped a page and smiled. "It seems that unicorns don't like pepper plants and are known to avoid them. I have a story here of Helga throwing a pepper at a unicorn and the thing running away in fear."

"Peppers? Where are we going to find pepper plants?" Jeff asked.

"My grandma grows hot peppers every summer, and she just made a big batch of homemade hot sauce. Do you think that would work?" Tiffany asked.

Mr. Hofstrom shrugged. "I think it's worth a try. It also says that, like horses, unicorns love apples, although they prefer to eat people. And that they prefer to hunt for people in open, grassy areas."

"Like the park?" Zach said. "My mom and sister were hanging out there last night and came back all goofy."

"Evie was talking about going to the park yesterday," Jeff said. "I bet they're there."

"There was that guy who was bitten by a weird

animal last week. I think he was in the park after dark. The police just thought he was on drugs," Tiffany said.

Mr. Hofstrom nodded. "I remember that guy. They thought he'd come from a party because he was covered in glitter. It all adds up."

"And the girl who got hit by the car yesterday," Zach said. "She was walking back from the direction of the park."

"Plus, I thought I saw Mason Briggs and the other missing kids at the park the other day," Jeff said.

"Also, I think I saw a unicorn there the day you guys showed me the sinkhole," Zach added. "But how do we get them to reveal themselves? It rained last night, but the sun has been out all morning, drying the grass."

They fell silent as they thought about it. After a few long seconds, Tiffany snapped her fingers and grinned. "I know! There are a couple of fire hydrants that drain right into the park. What if we got those opened?"

Mr. Hofstrom nodded. "I could call the mayor and get that done."

"We can get apples and the hot sauce. Using the apples as bait should attract most of the unicorns," Jeff said.

"And then we cover them with hot sauce and hope that sends them back where they came from," Zach said.

"Or blows them up," Tiffany said.

Zach's mouth hung open. "That seems kind of violent."

"Umm, they're trying to eat your family, remember?" she countered.

"Good point," Zach whispered.

Mr. Hofstrom grimaced. "I'll call the mayor and have the fire department open the hydrants at ten a.m. There's a note here that says the glitter only affects people when it touches their skin. So, it might be the magic, or you might be immune, or . . ."

"Or we might have just gotten lucky," Jeff finished.

Mr. Hofstrom pointed to the back of the library. "There's a lost and found bin. Make sure you're completely covered so that the glitter doesn't get you, in case you aren't immune or the Loyal Order of Helga magic doesn't work."

Tiffany nodded. "Thank you, Mr. H!" She and Jeff made to leave and Zach followed them to the lost and found bin.

"Mr. H isn't coming with us?" he asked, his voice low enough that the librarian couldn't hear.

"He can't leave the library," Jeff said.

"And no one knows why," Tiffany said. "I think he's cursed."

"I think he's scared," Jeff said. "He spent a long time living in the Otherside. Who knows what kind of scary stuff he had to fight off?"

"Have you asked him?" asked Zach.

"Of course. He refuses to talk about it," Tiffany said. "Either way, this is why we fight the monsters in Devils' Pass. Because someone has to," Tiffany said.

"And we're good at it," Jeff said with a grin.

Zach felt the stab of longing again. He was a little

surprised still at how much he wanted to be a part of the group. Not too long ago he thought they were just a bunch of weird kids.

He pushed the thought aside and dug through the lost and found bin, grabbing mismatched gloves and forgotten hoodies with Tiffany and Jeff. Once they were covered head to toe, Tiffany proclaimed them ready, and they left the library.

There were unicorns to fight.

CHAPTER THIRTEEN

Sparkle Ponies Really Know How to Party

Tiffany, Jeff, and Zach spent the rest of the morning preparing. Jeff had apples at his house, so they went there first. Evie and Ms. Allen were nowhere to be seen, and Jeff tried to hide his worry.

"They're probably at the park already," Jeff said.

No one said anything.

After spritzing the air with water to make sure there weren't any unicorns in the kitchen — since the water would reveal them — they cut up the apples carefully and put them in sandwich bags. Once they had a bunch, they put them in Tiffany's backpack and then headed to her house.

At Tiffany's house, she pulled out a two-gallon jar of hot sauce. Zach laughed. "That is a lot of hot sauce."

"Good hot sauce is hard to find," Tiffany said. "It's a shame we have to waste it on these stupid unicorns." She went out to the garage and came back with three oversized water guns. "I'm thinking we don't want to get any closer to the unicorns than we have to, since they have those teeth and horns. So, we can fill these with hot sauce and squirt them with it."

"Just be careful not to get it into your eyes," Jeff said, taking one of the squirt guns from Tiffany. "If you do, it'll totally burn."

"And then you'll be eaten by a unicorn," Zach said. "Don't forget that part."

"I don't think anyone can forget that," Tiffany said.

Once they each had a squirt gun full of hot sauce and a baggie full of apples, they headed to the park. It was already after ten o'clock. The park would be full of water when they arrived, the fire hydrants flooding the grass. Zach felt a few butterflies in his stomach, and he gripped his squirt gun harder.

When they got there, instead of water, the park was full of smiling townspeople. Worse, the grass was bone dry with no water in sight.

"Uh-oh. Something must've gone wrong," Tiffany whispered.

"The firefighters got glittered," Jeff said, pointing to a nearby fire hydrant. A firefighter stood next to it, covered in purple glitter. He held a giant wrench, a wide grin on his face.

"How are we supposed to see the unicorns now?" Tiffany said, her voice still low.

"And how do we even open the fire hydrants?" Jeff said.

"I know how to open them. At my old school, I spent a day following a firefighter around. She showed me how they open the hydrants. I'll get the fire hydrant, you two put the apples all over the grass, OK?" Zach said. "That way, when the grass floods, the unicorns will already be there." His heart pounded. Zach couldn't believe he was volunteering to do something so dangerous. All he wanted to do was run back home and hide under his covers.

"Ohmigod, look!" Tiffany whispered. In the middle of the grass, something was pulling a woman by her hair, dragging her toward the sinkhole. And whatever it was, that something was completely invisible. The woman wasn't even fighting —she smiled the whole time. "They must be trying to take everyone back to the Otherside."

"The unicorns are definitely here," Jeff said. "We have to do something now."

Somewhere in that crowd of people on the grass were Zach's mom and sister. He had to save them. Even if he was really, really scared.

"I've got this," Zach said, sounding more confident than he felt.

Tiffany nodded. "OK, be careful." She and Jeff moved toward the crowd of people. Tiffany's arms were loaded with apples and Jeff was carefully navigating the spaces on his crutches.

Zach tiptoed to the firefighter standing next to the fire hydrant. He didn't notice Zach, and when Zach waved his hand in front of the man's face, nothing happened. The firefighter was totally blissed out on unicorn glitter.

Not good.

Zach took hold of the giant wrench in the man's hand and pulled hard. He'd been expecting the firefighter to have a tight grip on the tool, and Zach was surprised when the wrench came free easily. The wrench was heavier than he'd expected, though, and it knocked him back a few steps. When he recovered his balance, Zach fitted the end of the wrench on the fire hydrant and twisted. At first, the cap that covered the pipe mouth on the front of the fire hydrant refused to budge, but then it released suddenly. It clanged loudly as it fell free, banging against the fire hydrant.

Neigh.

Zach froze as he heard the snuffle of a horse. He listened hard for clip-clopping hooves, but there was nothing except the sound of birds singing. There was no telling how close the unicorns were. He ducked deeper into the hood of his sweatshirt in case they were nearby.

Slowly Zach placed the wrench on the top of the fire hydrant and pulled. Like the front cap, the valve seemed stuck. But right when Zach began to worry that he wasn't strong enough, the valve opened up.

"Yes!" Zach said, raising the wrench into the air in triumph. The wrench was heavy, and threw him off balance so that he fell backward right into a puddle.

"Ugh," Zach said as he dropped the wrench and climbed to his feet. He saw Tiffany stifling a grin and he tried to ignore it.

The water came out hard and fast, knocking over a few folks standing too close to the hydrant. Zach ran over to help them, but luckily, they didn't seem to notice the water. It was easy to move them out of the way.

Suddenly he heard Tiffany yell, "Zach, look behind you!"

Zach turned around. He shouldn't have been celebrating. There were five very sparkly unicorns standing on the edge of the path near the fire hydrant.

And they looked very, very angry. One had a lot of red on its muzzle. Zach had a feeling he knew what that was.

His heart began to pound, and he could hear his pulse thrumming in his ears. He realized that he'd left his squirt gun next to the fire hydrant when he'd gone to help the people knocked over by the water. He had nothing to protect himself with. So, he did the first thing he could think of.

He ran.

Zach ran toward where he'd last seen Tiffany and Jeff. He weaved between townspeople he didn't know and some he did, like Mr. Gustaf, his geography teacher. He ran as fast as he could, his sneakers sloshing in the water that was very quickly flooding the park and streaming over the grass.

"Duck!" he heard Tiffany yell.

Zach hunched low to the ground. A stream of hot sauce flew over his head, and behind him he heard a whinny of rage. He saw Tiffany, shooting and pumping the squirt gun as quickly as she could. Zach dodged a dazed girl from his math class to get closer to her.

"I am so happy to see you!" He yelled to be heard over the angry whinnying.

"Be careful. It seems that the hot sauce does make them explode," Tiffany said.

Zach stood next to Tiffany and watched her squirt hot sauce at the unicorns. Sure enough, whenever the hot sauce touched them, the unicorns exploded into a cloud of glitter and confetti. The townspeople woke up as the unicorns exploded, and began to run and scream. Zach and Tiffany tried not to shoot them with the hot sauce, but every once in a while, someone would get it in their eyes or they'd fall on the wet, slippery grass. The combination of the people running around and the exploding unicorns made the park chaotic. It would almost have seemed festive if he didn't think about the unicorns eating everyone.

There were at least forty unicorns in the park, and the more the water spread through the grass, the more they saw. They all had different colors of hair, and each one of them exploded into a different shade of glitter and confetti as Tiffany directed her hot sauce at them. Zach watched the show, staying close to Tiffany, until she cleared her throat.

"Hey," she said, her voice low, as a few unicorns stalked closer to them. People were running in all directions, but the unicorns had stopped focusing on their dinner to focus on the current threat: Tiffany and Zach.

Tiffany said quietly, "I'm, um, almost out of hot sauce."

Zach looked at the squirt gun, and sure enough, the reservoir was almost empty.

"Where's yours?" she asked.

Zach pointed to the fire hydrant. There were at least four unicorns between them and his squirt gun, not to mention a handful of panicked people.

"This is bad," Tiffany said.

"Very bad," Zach said. He considered trying to make a run for his squirt gun, but the snarling unicorns and their very pointy teeth very quickly changed his mind.

"Well, bright side," Tiffany said. "At least we'll die happy?"

"Where's Jeff?" Zach asked.

"I haven't seen him since he went to find his mom and sister," Tiffany said.

Zach cupped his hands around his mouth. "Jeff! A little help!"

There was no answer, and between the enraged unicorns and the people freaking out all over the place, Zach couldn't see him anywhere.

Tiffany squeezed the trigger one last time, causing the closest unicorn to explode into a cloud of purple glitter. The remaining three stalked closer, their whinnies loud. Zach reached for Tiffany's hand and she gripped it tight, her face filled with fear.

"It's been really nice knowing you," Tiffany whispered.

"Really?" said Zach. And then added, "Ditto."

Zach closed his eyes as the unicorns squelched through the wet grass. He didn't want to see it coming when they ate him.

"YAAAAAAAAAAAA!"

Zach's eyes snapped open just as the unicorn nearest him burst into a cloud of green glitter. The glitter fell all over his face and skin, and he coughed. He tensed: at any moment he would start to feel . . . fine?

The glitter cleared, and Jeff grinned at Zach and Tiffany. "The glitter doesn't hurt you after you sauce them. Here." He held out Zach's squirt gun, and Zach took it as Jeff sighed. "There are a few left near the sinkhole. Last I saw, they were trying to jump the fence. I think they're going back to the Otherside."

"Did you find Evie and your mom?"

Jeff shook his head. "But I did find Zach's mom and sister. They're confused, but fine."

Tiffany nodded. "Take a break and go find Evie. We'll chase down the last few."

Jeff moved away, deeper into the park. Tiffany took Zach's squirt gun, dumped half of the hot sauce into hers, and smiled. "You ready?"

Zach nodded. "Let's sauce some sparkle ponies."

CHAPTER FOURTEEN

Welcome Home

Zach and Tiffany spent the rest of the morning chasing down and exploding the last few unicorns. By the time they returned to the park, everyone had woken up from their trances, the glazed looks leaving their faces as they did. As people returned to normal, they began to make their way back to their houses, laughing about what a great day it was.

No one seemed to think it was strange to be in the middle of the park at lunchtime on a Tuesday, wading through piles of glitter.

Zach found his mom and sister as the crowds began to thin. He hugged them hard — first his mom, and then Lisa.

"Hey. What's going on?" Ms. Lopez asked, laughing.

"I'm just really happy to see you," Zach said. Behind his mom, he watched as Jeff found Ms. Allen and Evie, and hugged them as well. Zach was happy to see that, like almost everyone else, the Allens looked fine. A few people had bite marks from unicorns that hadn't waited to start eating, but most of those folks had already been taken to the hospital by ambulances called by the firefighters.

Tiffany walked over, empty squirt guns slung over her shoulder. "Everything good?"

Zach nodded. He quickly introduced Tiffany to his mom, and Ms. Lopez frowned. "What time is it?" she asked.

"Lunchtime," Tiffany said. She bumped into Zach. "Come on, we have to get back to school. It's chicken à la king today. And I still have a bunch of stuff I need to get done for student council."

Ms. Lopez said, "Yes, we need to get back to class," and then moved toward the other people in the park.

"Wait, that's it? We just go back to school now?" Zach asked.

Tiffany grinned. "Yep. In a few minutes, everyone will forget what happened. Goldfish memory."

"What about us?" he asked. How could he forget about a unicorn eating his backpack?

"Oh, we'll remember. We always do. But everyone else?" She shrugged and pointed to the firefighters turning off the fire hydrant like nothing extraordinary had happened. "They'll forget. Their brains will reorder the events to be about drugs or a mountain lion attack, or something weird."

"There are mountain lions in Minnesota?" Zach asked.

Tiffany shrugged again. "Who knows? The important thing is that you'll remember. You're part of the Loyal Order of Helga now. I knew you would be the day we saw you sitting at our table in the cafeteria, drawing mermaids."

Zach's mouth fell open. "But how?"

Tiffany grinned. "No one ever sees the lunch table but Loyal Order members. Wonky magic, remember? Welcome to the club."

Zach blinked and a smile spread across his face. "Wait, what? Seriously?" The warmth spread all through him.

Jeff and Evie walked over, and Jeff nodded. "Oh, yeah. Once you've made it to the lunch table and helped fight off something from the Otherside you're definitely a member."

He grinned at Zach, and Zach grinned back.

"I can't believe I missed unicorns," Evie muttered.

"They were terrifying — you really should have seen them. The teeth alone . . ." Tiffany said. "But maybe Zach can draw you a picture, since he's such an awesome artist."

Zach looked at Tiffany to see if she was messing with him, but she wasn't. He grinned. "Yeah, totally. They had shark teeth."

Tiffany laughed. "And they ate Zach's backpack," she said, giving him a friendly smile.

"Wait, what am I supposed to do about my backpack? All my homework was in there, and the unicorn ate it," Zach said.

Tiffany laughed. "I guess you could always tell your teachers that your dog ate it."

"I don't even have a dog," Zach said with a grimace.

"You don't have a unicorn, either. Besides, which are people more likely to believe?" Evie said, smiling mischievously.

Jeff and Tiffany laughed, and Zach sighed.

Tiffany grinned and punched him in the arm affectionately. "Welcome to Devils' Pass," she said. "At least you know life will never be boring!"

UNICORNS

Origin: *Otherside*

Colors: *white body; golden horn; pink, blue, multicolor manes*

Likes: *apples, humans, large meadows, places to graze, lullabies, moving in herds*

Dislikes: *hot sauce, being made visible, being hungry*

Note on teeth: Unicorns have three rows of sharp, pointed teeth on their upper and lower jaws.

LOTS
OF
TEETH!!!

DON'T TOUCH
THE GLITTER!!!

This creature prefers grassy meadows and sparse woodlands. Unicorns feed exclusively on humans, most especially humans who are under exceptional amounts of stress. The beautiful, rainbow-hued manes of unicorns shed a metallic substance that looks like normal craft store glitter and immediately sends susceptible folks into a blissful state. Unicorns have several rows of very sharp teeth similar to a shark's. Unicorns are also one of the few monsters able to travel between the Otherside and the real world with ease.

They have been known to use their horns to stab those who are not subdued. Unicorns are invisible until their hooves get wet. When in the Otherside unicorns can be best avoided by wearing a necklace of peppers from the pickle pepper plant. Mr. Hofstrom's note: unicorns can be destroyed by a liberal application of hot sauce. Be warned that this leaves behind a very large pile of glitter (useful for sphinxes—don't forget to collect).

PEPPERS?

GLOSSARY

console – to make someone feel better

ditto – a copy of something; a way to say "me too"

furrow – to wrinkle

gape – to stare in disbelief

grimace – to make a face that shows displeasure

immunity – a resistance to disease or something contagious

indigenous – originating in a place; native

maneuver – to move in and out or around

muzzle – something to put around an animal's mouth to stop it from biting

remnants – pieces that are left from something

sass – to talk back or give an attitude

snippy – to be short or terse with someone

spritz – to spray lightly

stifle – to stop something from happening

Valkyrie – mythological handmaidens and warriors from Norse mythology

wonky – crooked or strange

YOU SHOULD TALK

1. Tiffany doesn't seem to trust Zach at first. What are some reasons you think she might not? What makes her decide to trust him toward the end of the book?

2. Zach decides not to tell the group about seeing flashes of a unicorn. Would you have told them? Why or why not?

3. Would you want to be a member of the Loyal Order of Helga? Why or why not?

WRITE ON

1. Write an email from Zach to one of his friends back in L.A. Now write an email back from that friend in response to Zach's email. Would Zach tell his friends about the LOH? If so, how would they react?

2. Pretend you are Mr. Hofstrom. What would you write in your notebook about unicorns? What are the important things to remember?

3. Write down what you think the Otherside looks like. What happens when you go through the sinkhole?

ABOUT THE AUTHOR

Justina Ireland lives with her husband, kid, and dog in Pennsylvania. She is the author of *Vengeance Bound* and *Promise of Shadows*, both from Simon and Schuster Books for Young Readers. Her forthcoming young adult book *Dread Nation* will be available in 2018 from HarperCollins and her adult debut *The Never and the Now* will be available from Tor/Macmillan. You can find Justina on Twitter as @justinaireland or visit her website, justinaireland.com.

ABOUT THE ILLUSTRATOR

Tyler Champion is a freelance illustrator and designer. He grew up in Kentucky before moving to New Jersey to develop his passion at The Joe Kubert School of Cartoon and Graphic Art. After graduating in 2010 he headed back south to Nashville, Tennessee, where he currently resides with his girlfriend and soon to be first kiddo. He has produced work for magazines, comics, design companies, and now children's books; including work for Sony Music, F(r)iction magazine, Paradigm Games, and Tell-A-Graphics. You can see more of his work at tylerchampionart.com.